Ursula Stillhart

When Dreams Come True

D1676562

Book Print Verlag

Bibliografische Information der Deutschen Bibliothek

Die Deutsche Bibliothek verzeichnet diese Publikation in der
Deutschen Nationalbibliografie;
detaillierte bibliografische Daten sind im Internet über
http://dnb.ddb.de abrufbar.

© Book Print Verlag, Karlheinz Seifried, 47574 Goch
Alle Rechte bei der Autorin: Ursula Stillhart
© Fotos: Ursula Stillhart
Satz: Heimdall DTP-Service, Rheine, dtp-service@onlinehome.de
Hergestellt in Deutschland, 1. Auflage 2008
ISBN: 978-3-940754-23-3

Book Print Verlag
Karlheinz Seifried
Weseler Straße 34
47574 Goch
http://www.verlegdeinbuch.de

When Dreams Come True

Ursula Stillhart

English Translation

Marsha Haechler-Luebbert

A special declaration of love
to my husband,
to my sister
and especially
to the Maldives!

Most girls and boys have their favorite stuffed animal that accompanies them throughout their childhood. It listens to their problems, consoles them, sleeps with them and shares their inner most secrets. In other words, these creatures are unconditionally always there when needed.

When these children become adults, finish their education and move out of their parents' home into their own apartment, these faithful companions are often forgotten. They get left behind in their mother's care. There they sit all alone and sad on the big empty bed, just patiently waiting to be needed again.
Some mothers feel sorry for these abandoned animals. And because they themselves are missing their children, they will sit down on the bed beside the animals, take them in their arms and give them a big loving hug.
Sometimes the bear, kitten, dog, or whatever animal it is, will start chatting with the mothers.
They begin to tell them about the past and about everything they experienced with the children. They relate stories of childhood pranks as well as fun and games. On top of that, they also know about the child's frustrations, whining and secret tears.
That is exactly what happened to the woman who is telling this story!

In her home two restless mice and a plump little horse were simply leftover. So she made herself comfortable in the children's room and started to talk to them about earlier times.
At some time or other she began to tell them about the fantastic vacation she had spent with her sister. The little animals perked up their ears and listened attentively as they heard about

-- the small islands in the Indian Ocean called the Maldives.
-- the adventures while diving and snorkeling.
-- the delicious food.
-- the cat that lives in this little paradise.

They became very curious and wanted to know precisely what it was like in this place where the summer never ends. Where the water and the sky are the very same blue, so that you can barely see the horizon dividing the one from the other. And where there are so many beautiful and colorful fish, that you could think you were swimming in an aquarium.

They begged and begged and didn't let up until they were promised that all three of them could go along the next time the woman went to this island.

Then one day they were all ready to go.
However, when the little horse found out that they had to travel by plane, he suddenly didn't feel very well. He insisted on sleeping in the suitcase until they reached their destination. A big surprise for each mouse was a suitcase with wheels, so they could pack their own things for the trip.

At last our wonderful vacation can begin!

How long is it still going to take? Our airplane isn't even here yet!

Stop! Wait! We're not traveling with the luggage, but with the people on the plane!

Look! Our suitcase is being loaded there too. I wonder how the little horse is feeling.

Why is he taking so long to board the plane? We want to finally get going!

Do YOU understand this? Someone has to help us. We can't fasten our seatbelts like the adults!

We only eat salad!
And why do they have fish on this plate?
Some cheese would be a lot better!

Whoa! The music is rushing right through us!
Afterwards, let's change the channel and listen to a fairy tale.

Imagine that! Just like home! We always have to dry the sink after washing our hands there too!

Do you think the two of us will really be able to sleep here? It sure isn't the same as being in our own bed! I guess, the main thing is to have sweet dreams, right?

Since we woke up so early, we can watch the sun rise!

No doubt about it, I bet we're the first mice ever to get to sit on the armrests of the pilot's and co-pilot's chairs.

NOBODY has ever been able to sit like this on an airplane!
We are the only ones in the whole wide world!

Can we stay here for a while if we sit in this corner and are as quiet as a mouse!

From up here we can see exactly what the pilot is doing. He really has to concentrate so he doesn't make any mistakes and nothing happens to our plane.

Are pilots supposed to understand this whole panel? Look at all of these buttons and knobs! How long do you have to go to school and study to become a pilot?
That must be a very difficult occupation!

Hey! Be careful! That's the joystick! It's the steering wheel of the airplane. We don't want to suddenly fly in the wrong direction!

This book shows exactly where we have to fly. All the pilots have to follow these air routes precisely. No one can just fly wherever they feel like flying, otherwise two airplanes might hit each other. What could happen then is something we'd rather not think about.

We are the little princes of the sky!

Let go of that cord! The pilot can order a cup of coffee or something to eat from the flight attendant with this telephone.
I think that's true, anyway. Unfortunately, he didn't have any time right now to explain what this phone is used for.

Look! The ocean is down there! Should I tell you how I feel? LIKE AN EAGLE! When it's flying, an eagle sees the earth just like this. Thank you very much, that we were able to visit the cockpit and look at everything up close.

How beauuuuuutiful!! Down there are the Maldives with its many many islands!

Could one of those vacation islands be ours?

How do the people know which direction to go?
There's only water as far as you can see!

It's a good thing the captain has a cell phone so that he can call the island and let them know we're coming!

Are we that excited? This wonderful island looks all blurry!
The sky and the water really are the same color blue!
And the sand is soooo white, as white as the snow at home.

Look, the palm trees and the sky are being reflected in this house number plaque.

This house would be just the right size for us! However, it's a lantern that shines at night so everyone can find their way home.

The Maldivian people have their own official language called Dhivehi. When we try to say their numbers, they sound a bit strange to us.

It isn't the same time as at home either. The Maldives are three hours ahead of central Europe.

SUCH A HIT! Our own little deck chairs made especially for mice on vacation.

Is it just my imagination, or are the waves coming a little closer each time they roll in?

Get off! You've got your own chair. But if you want to trade, we can.

I think it's time we finally choose. Do you want the red one or the blue one?

See! It's ok here! The water can't get us and there's plenty of space.

Say, are you sure you have to read your school book HERE and NOW? I have a much better idea!

What do you think? Would digging in the sand for two days be enough to reach the other side of the world? Where would that be?

Do you also want to know what everything looks like under water? OK! Then, let's go swimming!

It's not even deep here!   WOW! There's a huge fish!

That's a parrotfish. It's called that, because its mouth looks like a parrot's mouth.

You're called the velvet surgeonfish. You sure do look as smooth as velvet!

You just can't stop looking, there's so much to see! Although, the water does burn your eyes a bit, at least the eyes of mice!

I hope that every fish swimming by under us realizes that we aren't trying to catch fish with our tails.

Should we count the clouds? Of course just the ones that are directly over us!

Close your eyes and just enjoy the swirling and the rocking! We can forget all our little worries.

And now, where is the pier all of a sudden? All you can see is the roof of the little reception house far away!

I am a bit frightened being out this far. If we kick real hard with our legs, the ripples can help us get back to shore.

Is that a real diver's mask? And how do you snorkel?

Hey, this is fun! Our little horse always has the best ideas! The flippers would be ideal boats for us and we could use the snorkel as a paddle!

This isn't going to work. These things are ten times too big for us! We wouldn't be able to breathe with them under water or see anything at all!

Please let us down! Actually, we do know we shouldn't get into other people's things.

Help do the cleaning? That's supposed to be a punishment? Not for me! While cleaning I found something that can only be for little mice!

We are really being treated special! Miniature snorkel equipment, just for us!

Lying on this big flip-flop is perfect. We can snorkel without having to swim!

This works much better! The ocean water makes us float as if we were as light as little feathers.

Look at all the little striped fish under us! Whenever I try to swim closer to them, they hide.

Would one of you like to swim a race with me, or do you always swim in schools?

Now, which is the sky and which is the ocean? What I've heard is true! Both of them are the same blue, so that you can hardly tell the difference!

NO! You can't play beach volleyball with just two players. That isn't nearly as much fun.

We can't play water tennis either! We are just too small and the rackets are simply too big!

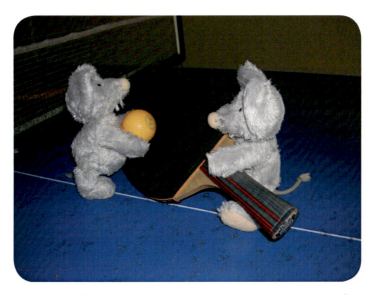

Finally! Now we found something we can play. This is perfect!

What a tiger! Lucky for us it's just painted on the wall! If it weren't, we'd really be in trouble!

Would you quit fooling around, so we could finally start our fussball match!

Don't act so goofy! Get onto the table and kickoff, or are you afraid of losing?

Do you want to bet I'll make a goal! And if I win, we'll share a pineapple juice up on the deck overlooking the ocean!

This glass full would be enough for four mice! Do pineapples actually grow on this island?

I was told that only coconuts and sometimes bananas grow in the Maldives. Everything else has to be shipped in from far away!

We sure lucked out again! This island has bananas. They're only little ones, but are THEY good!

Look at that big ship out on the water! It's bringing everything that is needed to the island. It's bringing all the food and beverages, the fruit, salad and vegetables, the meat and cheese as well as the milk and butter. But mainly it's bringing huge amounts of drinking water.

By the time you finish drinking your juice, your omelet is going to be cold! Next time don't take so much. Then you can finish everything on your plate. There is really enough there, so that you can always go back for more.

Did you do that on purpose? Now you're stuck! Why do you always have to have your nose into everything?

Does one have to use chopsticks to eat Chinese vegetables? If you don't know how to use them, it could really be frustrating.

I'd even like spinach, if I could only eat with a fork again!

Careful! This pan is hot! The chefs on this island know how to cook special dishes from all over the world. Today we're having an Italian meal!

Who can answer our question? Why do the slices of pineapple we buy at home have a whole in the middle? The middle piece are a bit harder, but still taste good and juicy.

Brrrrrrrr! Is it ever cold in here, just like at home in the winter! What is orange mousse? Is there really an orange mouse in there?

Open your mouth! First we'll have a bite of watermelon and then some peach cake!

Mmmm…! That tops it all! Passion fruit! The king of desserts!

Yes, yes, I know. After so many desserts, you have to brush your teeth. I don't really like doing that, but I'd rather have nice white teeth in my mouth than ugly black stubs.

That's great that you can read! That means we can still have our bedtime story even on vacation!

How do they do that? That bed looks so majestic! Just imagine how good we're going to sleep tonight!

There! Now the flowers have some water! By tomorrow morning they would have been all wilted and shriveled up!

Every night there are showers of blossoms and seedpods from the trees. And every morning they get swept up. Today we even get to help!

Somebody snitched our big orange blossom! It would have looked so pretty in our bed of flowers!

Camouflaged like this, no one will find me! You have to look twice before you can see me!

Aren't I camouflaged too? If not, at least I add to the picture!

This tree has thousands of hearts, in every size!

Have you got any idea, why that fence is there?

Oh, now I see! There are baby palm trees in there! This fence protects them so that they can grow without getting hurt.

Our help is needed to set a young plant in this pot.

Why can't we eat this coconut? Because it is already extremely old and it got washed up on our shore by the ocean!

But if it can float as well and as far as you say, then we could use it as a boat.

Even with a paddle, it doesn't want to budge. Well, let's just pretend we're out on the ocean.

Look! Down there are those big shy crabs! They hide the second anybody comes.

Stay here! I just want to watch you. I'm not afraid of you, although you do have many more legs than I do!

Oh, you poor little thing! Some big fish must have been awfully hungry. All that's left of you is your shell. Too bad, but even that's life!

Do you know why these crabs all look different? Because each one has to find an empty shell of its own to live in. And there are no two shells exactly alike in the whole world.

Now I understand what kind of tracks these are. Evidently a crab conference took place under this palm tree!

Look me in the eye, little guy! You know, we both have the same button eyes!

Wow, are you ever strong! That's quite a feat, climbing up there carrying your own house.

That's not very nice! You shouldn't pinch tender noses!

I'm sure this tiny thing won't hurt me. I just have to get a look up close at such a unique face as this.

PUT ME DOWN RIGHT NOW! We are too fragile to be touched, picked up or even carried around.

If we're very quiet and have a lot of patience, we can find out what made this pile of sand.

See! There it is! Every night the shore is covered with water. And every morning, when it is all dry again, these crabs dig themselves new tunnels.

Hello, there! Are YOU ever huge! Your legs look like strawberries. Shouldn't you be in the water? Or are you on shore to look for a new empty shell? Yours is very pretty, but much too small.

You live dangerously! You don't even have enough room in your shell to hide yourself completely.

Well then, good-bye and good luck! I hope you find an empty shell in the ocean so that you can live safe and sound for many many years.

Look here! There's air in these tanks. The divers can breathe under water with them and make millions of bubbles.

Today I get to go diving for the very first time in my life. Actually, I'm really looking forward to it, but my little heart is pounding like crazy because I'm so excited.

Oh, I hope this all goes well! Swimming with this equipment isn't as easy as it looks. Yippee!!! Over there I can already see the first fish!

In all of my little mouse life I have never seen anything as beautiful as this.

Real coral skeletons! What a natural work of art!

Giant clams! And as soon as you get close, they clam up!

Hello, little fish! I know that you live in a sea anemone. Yours is a marvelous specimen.

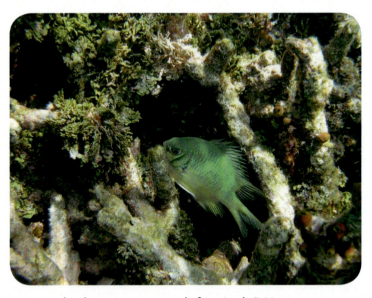

Why are you looking at me so defensively? Have you got something in those branches that you're protecting?

And you? Do you live amongst these stones? Say, why are you looking at me like that? Haven't you ever seen a mouse?

Yes, I know I'm in your territory. But if I want to see everything, I have to be able to get a little closer!

You don't even need to try to nibble at me. You can't eat me. I'm not edible.

I dub thee "little sun of the ocean"! Are you a long-nosed butterfly fish? There are so many different butterfly fish; it's difficult to tell you all apart.

Why are you called a cornet fish? You look like a flute to me!

Are you nibbling at that? Doesn't that hurt your teeth? Are you really getting enough to eat?

Because I'm so tired from diving, I get to ride back to shore in the FLIPPER-BOAT! Sometimes there are advantages to being so small.

I'll swim the last stretch. Not everyone has to know that I needed a little help.

Here's where the divers leave their empty air tanks when they get back. Someone from the diving school comes to get them and fills them up again for the next dive.

Today we were given some real Maldivian money, called RUFIYAA, so that we can buy ourselves a souvenir.

I'd like to change clothes to go shopping. Will you wait for me?

You have to hurry though, because we are taking a boat over to the capital city to go shopping.

The capital city is called Malé and it's also an island. The houses are built right up to the water because so many people live on this piece of land.

We're ready for our shopping spree! Hold me tight, or the wind will blow us across the ocean.

We were smart! We didn't buy anything that comes out of the ocean!

We DIDN'T buy any big shells or clams, NOTHING made out of turtle shells, and NOTHING made out of coral! Those things all have to stay in the ocean!

This fish looks as if it were real and it's a wonderful souvenir, isn't it! We're bringing it to someone we really like a lot.

That was a great buy! It's called a pareo, or sarong. With all this material you can always dress yourself a new way.

The Maldives are printed on our piece of fabric, the atolls and all of the vacation islands. At home we can show everyone exactly where we were.

We'd love to keep this butterfly fish, but it has to stay here. It belongs to this island!

It actually has to stay in its glass showcase. It can only come outside for a quick picture with us.

Have you ever seen anything like this? A shower without a roof!

Hello, Horse! Can I turn on the water? Will you catch me if I slide down the jet of water?

LA-LA-LOUSE! I think I hear a mouse! Oh, yes, just come! It's a lot of fun down here!

Don't squeal so loud! Everyone can hear you all over the island! Hey, come! I've got a great idea!

Nobody will believe us, when we tell them that there are no roofs over the showers in the Maldives. And that while we were sloshing around we could see the sky and the palm trees.

If I have to dry your back, then I get to mess up your fur some too!

We'll never manage this alone! Are you sure that this funny looking thing is a hairdryer?

Super! Just like at a beauty shop: sit still, wait a while, and you've got a lovely new hair-do!

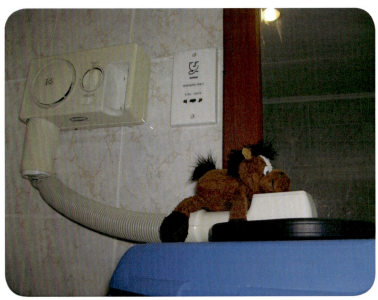

I like being a good friend and helping whenever I can, but sometimes those two little mice can sure wear me out!

Sit still! This doesn't hurt at all! After snorkeling or diving, everyone should rinse out their ears in the shower and put diver's drops into them.

As there are very tiny organisms in the water that don't belong in your ears, these drops will prevent you from getting an ear infection. Everyone knows, vacations and earaches don't go well together!

Thanks a lot that you are always there for us! We love you soooo much!

There was someone here before me! A GIANT! His feet are bigger than all of me put together!

Morning exercises before sunrise! That's very healthy!
ONE-TWO!   ONE-TWO!
INHALE - EXHALE!
INHALE - EXHALE!

Look over there! It looks like the sun is coming up right out of the water!

Which is going to be stronger, the sun or that big fat rain cloud?

That sure looks like rain! And there's really a strong wind blowing across the island.

We're already soaking wet! What will we do if it rains so hard that the ocean isn't big enough for it all?
Hold on tight! I'll take you back to where it's dry.

Oh my, Horse! More water is coming out of you than out of the sky!

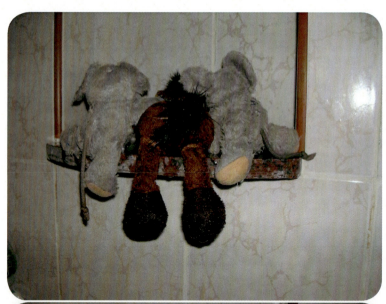

For once we can help YOU! You wouldn't make it alone!

That was fun! Two kinds of weather in one day! Now there's not a rain cloud around!

I can't stay put! The little waves keep swirling me around back-and-forth!

How big is the ocean actually? You can see the other side of our lake. Here there's only water for as far as you can see.

I bet I can see further if I climb up here. I want to know for sure.

That's strange! That dark stripe along the horizon keeps getting wider, although nothing else is changing.

We can't help you. Mice can't see any farther with their eyes than a horse. BUT we have an idea!

OOOH, is this ever high up! Well, you know, it's the tallest palm tree on the island.

There! We've reached the highest viewing point. And everywhere you look, there's still just water all around us.

An ocean is just so immense that you can't see the other side! It makes us realize just how small we are.

Today we're just going to loll around. Listen to the ocean roar! Ahhh, it's just another perfect day!

Alone for a change! That's fun too! Have my thoughts to myself; can daydream and nobody bothers me.
Now, to celebrate I'm going to go for a walk!

HELLO, CAT!!! Are you real?

So kind of you not to hurt me! Are you on vacation too? Em, no! Dumb me! I've already heard about you!

Tell me! What's it like living on an island all the time? I'm sure you don't know what a mountain is. Do you only eat dry morsels like these here, or do you catch yourself a fish now and then?

Are you waiting for somebody? Oh, I know! You're waiting for other vacationers that come here regularly and bring you things you like!

You needn't lick your mouth. I'm really not edible. The only thing you'd get would be a horrible stomachache.

Those two furry gray animals over there are my two friends. I want it to stay that way! Do you understand me, CAT?

SSSHHH!!! Don't move! In a minute we'll know if this cat is as friendly as we've been told it is.

That positively knocks me out! This tom really doesn't seem to know that cats eat mice! Well, that surely doesn't matter. Actually for us, that's perfect!

Isn't this twig bothering you between your toes? If you sit real still, I'll get it out for you.

Wouldn't you like to go back to Switzerland with us? You could explain to all the cats there, that it really isn't necessary to eat mice!

Doesn't your heart start to beat a little faster when you see something as beautiful as this? You could think the sun was going to fall right into the water.

Is there another horse like me somewhere in the whole wide world? It'd be nice to have a friend that looked similar to me!

Early tomorrow morning I'm going to ask the sun where the other side of the ocean is. THERE, where it's going down, I bet it can see it!

Where we live it takes a lot longer to get dark in the evening. Here it goes so fast because the sun is really below the horizon and not just behind a mountain!

SHHH! Quiet! Don't move! The heron is preying on a fish!

Nuts to you! Can't you sit still for just a minute? Herons fly away the second they hear a strange noise. I would have loved to see it catch a fish.

Hello, you little ants! There's nothing here for you to eat!

I better not move! Where did this bird come from all of a sudden? I've never seen him around here before.

You can have these crumbs! But I can let you in on where there are some ants! That'd be something for you!

Oh, I see. You're looking for food for your chicks! Good thing you're hiding them! Who knows what all could happen to them!

Didn't I tell you? This big pot makes a perfect swimming pool! A couple more blossoms and we could take a luxurious bath!

Now we can let ourselves drift as long as we want to and we'll still be in the same spot.

Come in too, Horse! It's a lot of fun! You're usually such a strong and brave horse! What's wrong now?

Just because someone is big and strong, doesn't mean they can do everything and aren't afraid of anything!

Come! Let's do something else! I think Horse is worried about something that he isn't telling us.

Now THIS suits me: drinking some sparkling water, enjoying the sun and just dangling my legs in the water. No one will notice I can't swim!

What's the deal here? Such a big special pineapple juice, just for me?

Do you want to help me drink this? It's probably a bit too much for me alone!

This vacation has been so terrific; I even forgot my own birthday!
Luckily, the people on this island think of those special days.

What a surprise; a real birthday cake! The waiters sang to me and congratulated me!

What a treat! We're in the middle of the Indian Ocean on a tiny little island and we're celebrating MY birthday!

We're sending off this spray of flowers from the table decoration on a long journey! In our minds we've given each blossom a wish to take along.

Can you still see the flowers? If anybody finds them, I'm sure all their dreams will come true!

We did so many wonderful things here! And now it's time to go home. Too bad that vacations always go by so fast!

Are you sure you don't want to sit with us on the plane? Traveling in the suitcase is so boring and we won't see each other until we get home!

Of course, we're glad to go home again, but we're also a bit sad to be leaving!

All aboard! Here we go! Our biggest wish is to come back here again sometime!

Look at how fast we're speeding past this island! Why are those houses standing in the water? Don't they get washed away?

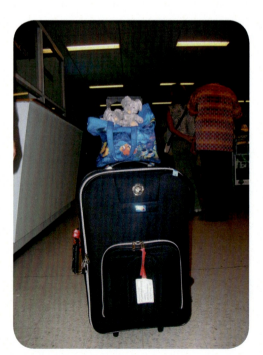

Are you always thinking about Horse too? I wonder how he is inside the dark suitcase. Next time he definitely has to ride with us on the plane!

Do you know what I'm looking forward to the most? A nice big hunk of cheese! Do you recognize those flowers on the airplane? We've got the same kind growing in our garden at home!

Even though the airport is an island with only one runway, our pilots will fly us back to Zurich safe and sound!

We'll show this ticket to everyone! Otherwise they might not believe us when we tell them WHERE we were and ALL we did!

Even for us it sometimes seems like it's all been a dream! The Maldives are so beautiful!

My sincere gratitude goes out to all who supported me in my project and believed along with me in my dream!